Presented

by

THE WOMAN'S CLUB
OF MT. LEBANON

- 2004 -

THE PAINTED WALL

The
PAINTED WALL
AND OTHER STRANGE TALES

Selected and Adapted from

the *Liao-chai* of Pu Sung-ling

by

MICHAEL BEDARD

Tundra Books

Copyright © 2003 by Michael Bedard

Published in Canada by Tundra Books,
481 University Avenue, Toronto, Ontario M5G 2E9

Published in the United States by Tundra Books of Northern New York,
P.O. Box 1030, Plattsburgh, New York 12901

Library of Congress Control Number: 2003100904

National Library of Canada Cataloguing in Publication

Bedard, Michael, 1949-
    The painted wall and other strange tales / Michael Bedard.

ISBN 0-88776-652-8

    1. Pu, Songling, 1640-1715 – Adaptations – Juvenile literature.
2. Ghost stories, Chinese.   3. Love stories, Chinese.   I. Title.

PS8553.E298P36 2003   jC813'.54   C2003-901301-4
PZ7

We acknowledge the financial support of the Government of Canada
through the Book Publishing Industry Development Program (BPIDP)
and that of the Government of Ontario through the Ontario Media
Development Corporation's Ontario Book Initiative. We further
acknowledge the support of the Canada Council for the Arts and the
Ontario Arts Council for our publishing program.

Design: Blaine Herrmann

Printed and bound in Canada

This book is printed on acid-free paper that is 100% recycled, ancient-
forest friendly (40% post-consumer recycled).

1   2   3   4   5   6   08   07   06   05   04   03

For
Bob Knowlton
Yishi shi

Acknowledgments

The English-speaking reader owes a great debt of gratitude to the pioneering translation of the *Liao-chai* by the noted sinologist Herbert A. Giles in 1908. Published as *Strange Stories from a Chinese Studio*, Giles's translation of 164 of the nearly 500 stories in the original collection remains the most substantial selection available in English and is the primary source for the stories in this collection. I have also consulted the fine translation by Rose Quong in 1946 of forty of the *Liao-chai* stories, under the title *Chinese Ghost and Love Stories*; and the tales translated by Yang Hsien-yi and Gladys Yang, which appeared in *Chinese Literature* (October 1962).

Contents

Introduction: Pu Sung-ling and the *Liao-chai*   1
Planting a Pear Tree   5
The Tiger of Chao-cheng   8
Princess Lily   12
Missing Silver   19
The Wonderful Stone   24
The Taoist Priest of Lao Shan   30
Pianpian, the Leaf Fairy   35
Past Lives   41
Paper Robes   45
Jen Shui, the Gambler   49
The Invisible Priest   54
The Man Who Was Changed into a Crow   57
The Glass Eyes   63
The Two Friends   65
The Talking Eye Pupils   71
Theft of the Peach   75
The Assistant to the Thunder God   79
A Case of Possession   85
A Supernatural Wife   93
The Pigeon Collector   96
The Arrival of the Buddhist Monks   101
The Magic Path   103
The Painted Wall   106

Introduction
Pu Sung-ling and the Liao-chai

More than a hundred years before the Grimm brothers began gathering their famous collection of folk and fairy tales in Europe, a similar collection had been compiled in far-off China by the scholar Pu Sung-ling. From a wide variety of oral and written sources, Pu had drawn together close to five hundred stories. He called his collection *Liao-chai chih-i* (Strange Tales from a Studio of Leisure). These stories of the strange and wondrous became as famous in China as the Grimms' stories did in the West. Indeed, the *Liao-chai* now holds the honor of being the most popular collection of stories in Chinese history.

Pu Sung-ling was a fascinating figure in his own right. He was born in Shan-tung Province in the northeast of China in 1640. His father was a moderately prosperous merchant and a devoted scholar who, at forty years of age, abandoned trade, took to his books, and devoted his life

1

to learning. His wealth dwindled; his estate declined; and when he came to divide his property among his children, his youngest child, Pu, was left with little more than a tumbledown shack on a barren bit of land.

Pu, like his father, was a scholar. At nineteen he won distinction by placing first in the county exams. However, he was destined to fail the rigid provincial exams repeatedly over the next forty years. As a result, he was denied a government appointment – and the wealth and honor that came with that. Consequently, he struggled with poverty all his life, supporting his family by taking on a variety of teaching positions with the families of the local gentry. Although he was an educated man, Pu's own hardships made him sensitive to the plight of the common people, and he shared their views on many things.

In the mid-seventeenth century, China was a country in turmoil. When Pu was five years old, the Ming dynasty fell and the Manchu invaders took power. During his lifetime, Pu witnessed a succession of peasant rebellions and the cruel repressions that followed. Corruption among government officials and the ruling gentry was widespread, and criticism was punishable by death.

In face of these bitter realities, Pu sought solace in writing. He wrote plays, poems, and works of popular education, but his fame rests squarely on his collection of supernatural tales, the *Liao-chai*. Such stories had always been popular with the common people, for they provided a brief respite from the hardships of their daily lives. For Pu they were a means of exercising his literary talents, expressing his frustrations, and criticizing the corruption around him under the guise of telling ghost stories.

He cast his stories in the style of classical Chinese literature, keeping to its ideals of balance and brevity, but bringing to it a new breadth of feeling, and striking a strong personal note not heard before. In his preface to the collection, Pu explains how the book began:

> I am driven by the spirit of Tung-po, who loved to listen to people tell ghost stories. What I have heard, I have put to paper, and dressed it up in the shape of a story. Over the course of time, friends from all parts of the country have sent me material and, out of my love of collecting, a great pile has arisen.

There are many collectors in these tales, as there are many students attempting to pass provincial exams; and there are a host of poor scholars and bookworms. The stories reflect both their author and the times in which he lived. They are characterized throughout by a vivid depiction of reality shot through with the strangeness of the supernatural. Pu Sung-ling wove together the realms of fantasy and reality so seamlessly that the supernatural seems natural, and the day to day is suddenly steeped in mystery.

※

The *Liao-chai* was the labor of a lifetime. Pu worked on the collection from the time he was thirty until he was well over seventy. When he died at seventy-five in 1715, the manuscript comprised eight volumes.

For many years after, only hand-copied versions of the stories were circulated. It was not until 1766 that the collection was first printed and published. It was an immediate success and went through numerous editions over the years. By the mid-nineteenth century, it had become so famous throughout China that one writer commented that "almost every household has a copy of the book."

Not only were the stories widely read, they became immensely popular with storytellers and their audiences. At the time, it was the custom for storytellers to perform in teahouses. For a small admission fee, one could sit for half the day, drinking tea and listening to tales of ghosts, fox fairies, and other wonders.

Imagine, then, a lazy summer afternoon. We have paid our coin and taken a table near the window, where a cool breeze blows off the river and the scent of lotus flowers perfumes the air. A motley crowd has gathered – men and women, young and old, rich and poor. The murmur of voices fills the room. There is a cup for me and a cup for you. The tea is steeping. Let the stories begin.

Planting a Pear Tree

A man was selling pears in the marketplace. They were sweet and fine flavored, and the price he was asking was high. A Taoist priest dressed all in tatters happened by and, stopping before the countryman's cart, begged a pear of him.

"Get away!" said the man. And when the priest failed to move along, he began to curse and swear at him.

"You have several hundred pears on your cart," said the priest. "Yet when I ask you for a single one, which you would not even miss, you grow angry."

By this time a crowd had begun to gather. The onlookers urged the countryman to give the priest a bruised pear and be done with it, but he refused. The bailiff of the market, finding the commotion getting out of hand, took out some coins and bought a pear, which he handed to the priest. The priest thanked him with a bow, then turning to the crowd, he said: "We who have given up our homes and all that is dear to us find it hard to understand stinginess in others. Now I have some exquisite pears, which I shall freely offer to you all."

"If you have pears of your own," said one of the onlookers, "why didn't you eat one of those?"

"Because first I need one of these pips to grow them from," said the priest. He made quick work of the pear, then took a pip in his hand and, unfastening a pick from his shoulder, made a hole in the ground several inches deep. He dropped in the pip, covered it with dirt, and asked one of the bystanders to fetch him a little boiling water, which he poured over it. All eyes were fixed upon him.

Suddenly a sprout shot up from the spot. It grew larger and larger, branched and thickened, and in a trice there was a full-grown tree laden with leaves before them. Buds appeared in rich profusion, then flowers, and finally all the branches were hung with fruit – plump, ripe, fragrant pears.

The priest began to pick them and hand them round to the crowd, until every last one was gone. Then he took his pick and began to hack away at the base of the tree. Finally it fell and he shouldered it, leaves and all, and walked quietly away.

All this time, the countryman with the cart of pears had been standing among the crowd, straining his neck to see, and forgetting all about his business. Now that the priest had disappeared from view, he turned – and saw that every last pear on his cart was gone! Instantly he realized that the pears the priest had been giving away were his.

Then he noticed that one of the handles had been lopped off his cart. He set off after the priest in a rage. Turning a corner, he found the cart handle abandoned at the base of a wall, and knew that this was the pear tree the priest had cut down and carried off. But as for the priest – he was nowhere to be found.

The Tiger of Chao-cheng

At Chao-cheng there lived an old woman over seventy, who had an only son. One day he went out hunting in the hills and was eaten by a tiger. His mother was overwhelmed with grief. She ran to the magistrate in tears and demanded that the tiger be brought to justice. He laughed aloud and asked her how she thought the law could be brought to bear on a tiger.

The woman would not be moved. The magistrate lost his temper and told her to leave. Still she would not stir. Finally, in deference to her age and to be done with her, he promised to have the tiger arrested.

The woman refused to go until a warrant had been issued. The magistrate, at his wit's end, looked around the room at his attendants and asked which of them would be willing to undertake the task of arresting the tiger. One of them, Li Neng, who had been up all night drinking with

8

friends, stepped forward and said *he* would. The warrant was immediately issued, and the old woman went away.

When Li Neng had sobered up a little, he regretted his rash offer. Still, he assured himself, the whole affair had been merely a trick of his master's to be rid of the old woman. He handed in the warrant as if the arrest had been made, and thought no more about it.

The next day the magistrate summoned him. "You promised you would arrest this tiger," he said. "And so you shall."

Li Neng felt his heart sink. He begged the magistrate to allow him to enlist the services of the hunters in the district. The request was granted. So he rounded up all the hunters he could find and spent day and night among the hills, hoping to catch a tiger – any tiger – and make a pretense of having fulfilled his duty.

⊰⊱

A month passed with no tiger to show for his labors. Several times Li Neng was called before the magistrate and caned for failing to fulfill his duty. Finally, in despair, he went off to a temple in the hills alone. Throwing himself down on the ground, he wept and prayed by turns. While he was thus engaged, a tiger walked in. Li Neng was filled with panic, convinced that he was about to be eaten alive. But the tiger sat calmly near the doorway, taking no notice of him at all.

Li Neng at last summoned the courage to speak to the creature. "O Tiger," he said in a tremulous voice, "if you are the one who killed the old woman's son, allow me to bind you with this cord." And taking a rope from his pocket, he threw it over the beast's neck. The tiger drooped its ears and allowed itself to be bound.

Li Neng led it to the magistrate's office. The magistrate asked the beast: "Did you eat the old woman's son?"

The tiger replied with a nod of its head.

"It has always been the law that murderers must suffer death themselves," the magistrate went on. "Besides, this old woman had but one son, and by killing him you have robbed her of the sole means of support in her old age. Nonetheless, if you will be as a son to her, your crime shall be pardoned."

Again the tiger nodded in assent, so the magistrate gave orders that it be released. The old woman was beside herself, claiming that the tiger ought to have paid with its life for the murder of her son.

⁂

The next morning, however, when she opened the door of her cottage, there was a dead deer lying before it. By selling the meat and the skin, the woman was able to buy food. And so it continued. Sometimes, the tiger would even bring her money and other valuables. And so, in the course of time, the woman grew rich and was much better taken care of than she had ever been by her son.

The two became friends. Often the tiger would come and doze away the whole day in the shade of the veranda, giving no cause of fear to man or beast. The years passed, and then one day the woman died. The tiger stood in front of the cottage and roared its grief.

No expense was spared in her funeral; it was a splendid affair. As the relatives were standing about the gravesite, in rushed the tiger and sent them all scattering in terror. But the tiger merely went up to the burial mound, gave one thunderous roar of farewell, and disappeared.

The people of that place built a shrine in honor of the Faithful Tiger. I believe it stands there still.

Princess Lily

In Chaio Chou there lived a man named Tou Hsun. One afternoon, while taking his nap, he was startled to find a man dressed in brown standing by his bed. The man seemed anxious to speak to him.

"Who are you?" demanded Tou.

"I am the bearer of an invitation from my master," said the man.

"And who might your master be?"

"A neighbor of yours, my lord."

So Tou went with him and in a short time they came to a place set in the shade of a lemon grove, where countless white houses rose one above another. They passed through many strange doors and saw crowds of men and women dressed in court clothes and bustling busily about. When the people saw the man in brown, each of them asked if Mr. Tou had come. To which he replied: "Yes, he has."

At length a court official met them and escorted Tou into a palace. Two maidens with banners appeared and guided Tou through many more doors, until they came at length to a room where a prince sat upon a throne. When he saw Tou, the prince rose to welcome him and showed him to the seat of honor.

Tou was deeply puzzled by all this, and said: "My lord, I cannot think why you should receive me, a stranger, with such favor."

"I have heard you are a man of virtue," said the prince. "As we are neighbors, a bond of affinity exists between us. Let us put aside doubts and fears and give ourselves over to enjoyment."

Tou readily agreed. The wine went round several times, and from within, Tou heard the muffled sound of music. Then, with a tinkling of jeweled pendants and the delicious odor of musk, there came into the room the most beautiful girl Tou had ever seen.

"This is my daughter Lily," said the prince.

She bowed and smiled.

Tou was so overcome by her beauty that he was in a daze and did not hear the prince when he raised his cup and proposed another drink. At length the girl withdrew; whereupon, the prince said: "I am seeking a husband for my daughter. It is sad she is not of your kind, but what can be done?"

Still Tou seemed not to hear. It was not until a courtier standing nearby tugged at his sleeve that he recovered himself. Then, embarrassed, he rose. "Forgive me, my lord, but I fear I have taken too much wine. It is late and no doubt there is much business to which you must attend, so I will take my leave."

The prince said he was sorry that Tou had to go so soon. "But if you do not completely forget us, I shall be glad to invite you again."

On the way home, the courtier who was escorting Tou asked him why, when the prince had spoken about seeking a husband for his daughter, he had remained silent, since it was obvious the prince had Tou in mind for a son-in-law. At this, Tou cursed himself for having missed his opportunity. Then they reached home . . .

. . . And Tou awoke. The sun was setting, and he sat long in the falling dark, reflecting on all that had happened in his dream. Late that night, as he put out the candle in his room, he prayed that the dream would return. But the way had closed, and all he could do was sigh with the loss of it.

❧

One night some time later, Tou happened to be sleeping at the house of a friend, when suddenly the courtier appeared before him and said that the prince had summoned him to the palace. Tou followed him eagerly, and when they came to the throne room, he prostrated himself before the prince. The prince raised him up and led him again to the seat of honor.

"Since last we met, I have been given to understand that you would be willing to marry my daughter," he said.

Tou replied that indeed he would, so the prince ordered that a great feast be prepared. All the members of court were in attendance. After the wine had been poured, it was announced that the princess had completed her preparations. A group of young ladies entered the room, and there she was in their midst. A red veil covered her head, and as she glided across the room to greet Tou she seemed hardly to touch the floor.

When the wedding ceremony was completed, the couple were shown to their chamber.

"With you standing here before me, I could forget even death," said Tou. "But tell me, dear one, is this all a dream?"

"We are here together," the princess said. "How could it be a dream?"

❈

When they awoke the next morning, Tou amused himself by helping his bride with her makeup. He took her sash and measured the size of her waist, and with his fingers he measured the length of her foot.

"What are you doing?" she laughed.

"I have been deceived by dreams too often," he said. "I am taking careful note of all, so that should this, too, prove to be a dream, I will have a clear remembrance of you."

At that moment a maid rushed into the room.

"A monster has entered the palace," she cried. "We shall all be killed!"

Tou rushed to the prince, who took his hand and, with tears in his eyes, begged him not to abandon them.

"But what has happened?" asked Tou.

The prince pointed to a letter on the table and told Tou to read it. It was from Black Wings, the secretary of state. It read:

A report has been received from the guardian of the Yellow Gate, stating that since the sixth day of the fifth month, a great monster – more than ten thousand feet in length – has lain coiled outside the palace gate. Already it has slain more than thirteen thousand of Your Highness' subjects and is spreading ruin everywhere.

Upon receiving this report, your servant immediately investigated and discovered a terrible serpent, with a head as huge as a mountain and eyes like sheets of ice. Each time it spread its jaws, whole buildings disappeared down its throat; when it tightened its coils, walls crumbled and houses fell in ruins. It is only a question of hours before our temples and ancestral halls will fall to the same fate.

We advise the immediate removal of Your Highness and the royal court to a place of safety.

As he finished reading the letter, Tou's face turned ashen. At that moment a messenger rushed in. "The monster is here!" he shrieked.

The whole court fell to wailing, and the prince himself trembled with fear. He urged Tou to save himself, for it was only through his daughter that he had been caught up in their misfortune. But the princess begged Tou not to desert her.

"I possess no palace," he said. "But if you would humble yourself to take refuge in my poor dwelling, I would be honored."

"How can you talk of humbling at a time like this?" she asked. She took his arm and fled with him from the palace.

In little time they came to Tou's house. The princess looked about and was well pleased with the place, saying it was even better than the palace. "But what are we to do about my parents? I beg you to make arrangements for them as well, that the kingdom may continue here."

"But how is that possible?" said Tou, looking around his two small rooms.

"Of what use is a man who will not aid another in his time of need?" wailed the princess. She threw herself on the bed and burst into a fit of crying. Try how he might, she could not be consoled. . . .

. . . At that moment Tou awoke in the house of his friend. All had been a dream. But the sound of wailing was still in his ears, though it now seemed hardly a human cry. He looked about and found three bees buzzing beneath his pillow. He called out to his friend and told him all that had happened, and he, too, was amazed.

They rose then and the friend noticed, clinging to Tou's clothing, a number of bees that refused to be brushed away. He advised him to obtain a hive for them, which he did without delay, and immediately a great swarm of bees came flying up over the wall and filled the hive.

On inquiring as to where they might have come from, they found that an old man who lived nearby had been keeping bees in his lemon grove for more than thirty years. Tou went and told him his story, whereupon the old man examined the hives. He found that one of them was without bees and, breaking it open, he discovered a large snake more than ten feet long coiled about the inside. Recognizing it as the monster of Tou's dream, the old man killed it instantly.

As for the bees, they remained with Tou and flourished with the passing years.

Missing Silver

One day the governor of Hu-nan sent one of his magistrates to the capital, in charge of six hundred thousand ounces of silver to be paid as tribute to the emperor. As they were traveling, the magistrate and his party ran into a violent storm and were unable to make the next way station before nightfall. They took shelter in an old temple. When morning broke, the magistrate discovered to his horror that the treasure was gone.

Unable to fix guilt on any of the party that accompanied him, he returned immediately to the governor and told him the whole story. The governor refused to believe him and would have had the magistrate severely punished but for the fact that all who had traveled with him supported the magistrate's story. Therefore the governor sent them all back to search for the missing silver.

When they arrived at the temple, they encountered a strange-looking blind man who told them that he could read people's thoughts, and that they had come there on a matter of money.

"Indeed, it is so," said the magistrate, and he went on to tell the story of the missing treasure.

"If you follow me you will find it again," said the blind man. So the magistrate called for a sedan chair to carry the man, and he and his party followed after him according to the directions he gave them. If the man said east, it was east they went; if north, then they all turned north. In this way they wound through mountainous country for five days until they came at last to a large city. They entered the gates and passed through the crowded streets for a short distance.

"Stop here," said the blind man, and he climbed down from the sedan chair, pointed to a great door, and told the magistrate to make his inquiries there. Whereupon, he bowed low, took his leave, and disappeared into the crowd.

The magistrate knocked upon the door, which was opened at length by a man dressed in the ancient style of the Han dynasty, which had come to an end nearly two thousand years before. The magistrate explained why he had come, and the man told him that if he would wait a few days he could assist him in the matter. He invited him inside, gave him a room, and brought him food regularly. And so the days passed.

❧

One morning the magistrate decided to take a walk, and venturing out the back door, found himself in a beautiful garden. There was an avenue of pines flanked on either side by wide smooth lawns, set with arbors and ornamental statues. He wandered along the avenue, and came upon an old stone summerhouse. Walking up the steps, he discovered to his horror, hanging there on the wall, a number of human skins, each with eyes, ears, nose, mouth, and heart.

He ran back to his room and shut himself in, dreading that the same fate awaited him. Yet, seeing little hope of escape, he decided to see what would happen.

The next morning the man who had let him in came back and told him that he could now have an audience with his master. He led him at length into a chamber where a king, wearing a cap set with pearls and an embroidered sash, sat upon a throne. The magistrate rushed forward and flung himself upon the ground before him. The king asked if he was the official who had been charged with the transport of the treasure of silver. The magistrate said he was indeed the man.

"The money is here," said the king. "It is not much, but I am pleased to receive the gift of it from the governor."

"Please, Your Majesty," pleaded the man. "If I return again empty-handed, I shall be punished by death."

"Take this then," said the king. And he put into his hand a thick sealed letter. "Give this to the governor, and no harm will come to you." He provided an escort for the magistrate and his party, who led them by another way than they had come and left them where the hills ended.

In a few days they were safely home. The magistrate went to the governor and explained all that had happened.

Again the governor refused to believe him. He ordered the man bound hand and foot and carried away. But before the order could be carried out, the magistrate took the letter from his coat and handed it to the governor. When the governor broke the seal and opened the letter, his face turned ashen. He gave orders that the magistrate be released, and told him he was free to go. He commanded his ministers to make up the missing money by whatever means and send it immediately to the capital. Then he took to his bed, deathly ill.

∻

Shortly before the events narrated here, it had happened one morning that the governor's wife had awakened to find all her hair gone. The entire household had been shocked and dismayed at such a strange occurrence. Now when the governor opened the letter, he found inside it his wife's hair along with these words:

Ever since you took office, your boundless greed has led you to embezzle public funds. The six hundred thousand ounces of silver are safely stored in my treasury. Make good these funds from the money you have stolen. The man you have charged is innocent; release him immediately. On a former occasion, I took your wife's hair as a gentle warning. I return it

22

now as evidence of what I say. If you fail to follow my instructions, I will have your head.

The governor did not recover from his illness. After he died, the family revealed the contents of the letter. A party of men was sent out to search for the city, but they found only range on range of towering mountains, with no trace of a road or trail.

The Wonderful Stone

There once lived a man named Hsing, a mineralogist, who would pay a handsome price for a good specimen. One day while he was fishing in the river his net became entangled, and diving down to free it, he brought up a stone about a foot in diameter, beautifully carved to resemble a clustering of hills and peaks.

He was delighted with his find and had a sandalwood stand made for it, upon which he displayed the piece. Now, the stone had a marvelous quality to it, for whenever it was about to rain, clouds would come forth from each of the holes and grottoes in it and appear to close them up.

Word of the wondrous stone spread far and wide and soon a steady stream of visitors was calling at Hsing's house, hoping to see it. Fearing for the safety of the stone, Hsing had it removed to an inner room and hidden there.

The Wonderful Stone

Some time after, an old man knocked at the door and asked to see the stone. Hsing said he had lost it long ago.

But the old man said: "Is that not it in the inner room?" At which he entered the house and walked directly to the room where the stone was hidden. Hsing was very much taken aback by this.

The old man laid his hand on the stone and said: "This is an old family relic of mine, which I lost many months ago. How did it come to be here? I pray you give it back to me."

"But the stone is mine," protested Hsing.

"What proof have you that it is yours?" asked the old man.

Hsing made no reply.

"To prove that it is mine," said the old man, "I will tell you that there are altogether ninety-two grottoes in the stone, and in the largest of these are written the words *A Stone from Heaven above.*"

Hsing counted the number of grottoes and found that there were indeed ninety-two, and in the largest of these, written in letters so small they could hardly be seen, he found the words the old man had said were there. But still he would not part with the stone.

The old man laughed and asked, "Pray tell me, what right you have to keep other people's things?" He bowed and turned to go.

Hsing saw him to the door, but on returning to the room he found that the stone was gone. Amazed at this, he ran after the old man, caught him by the sleeve, and begged him to give back the stone.

"And do you think I could conceal so large a stone in my sleeve?" asked the old man.

But Hsing knew that this must be a supernatural being, and he begged that he might have the stone back.

"Is it mine or yours?" asked the old man mildly.

"It is yours," said Hsing, "though I hope you will deny yourself the pleasure of keeping it."

"The wonders of this world should be given to those who know how to take care of them. I am pleased that the stone should remain with you. It is back again."

Hsing returned to his house with the old man, and in the inner room they found the stone in its place again.

"There is one thing more," said the old man. "The number of grottoes in the stone stand for the length of your life. Should you choose to keep it here, the span of your life will be shortened by five years. Are you willing that this be so?"

Hsing said that he was, whereupon the old man touched the fingers of one hand to the stone. The stone melted like wax where the fingers touched, and five of the holes were sealed shut. Then the old man bowed and went upon his way.

❧

Several years passed, and the stone sat safely in the inner room, and when it was about to rain, clouds would issue magically from the grottoes.

One day Hsing was called away on business, and while

he was gone, a thief broke into his house and stole the stone. When Hsing returned, he was deeply grieved. He inquired everywhere, but was unable to recover it.

Then, on his way to the temple one day, he noticed a man selling stones, and among them was his own. He told the man that the stone was his and had been stolen from him, but the stone seller refused to part with it.

Hsing took his case to the nearest magistrate. The magistrate asked him how he could prove the stone was his, whereupon Hsing told him the number of grottoes that were hollowed in it, and told him the words he would find written in the largest of them. Hsing won the case, and the stone seller was dismissed.

But the magistrate had taken a fancy to the wonderful stone, and offered to buy it from Hsing for one hundred ounces of silver. Yet Hsing said that he would not part with it for even ten times that sum.

At this the magistrate became so enraged that he trumped up a false charge against Hsing and had him thrown into prison. The official then sent someone to Hsing's wife and son, offering to release him in return for the stone. When Hsing heard of this, he begged them not to give it over, saying that he and the stone must not be parted, even in death.

Nevertheless, the family sent the stone to the official to win his release. On his return home, discovering that the stone was gone, Hsing was cast into a deep despair. But in the midst of his despair, he had a dream. In the dream a noble-looking person appeared before him and said:

My name is Shih Ch'ing-hsu (Stone from Heaven). Do not grieve. I have purposely left you for a time, but next year, on the twentieth day of the eighth moon at dawn, come to the city gates and you may buy me back for two strings of cash.

Hsing was overjoyed and took careful note of the day mentioned in the dream.

Meanwhile, the stone was displayed in the magistrate's house. But the magical clouds no longer appeared, and so it grew less and less prized. In the following year, the magistrate was charged with corruption and subsequently died. His servants were sent off with the stone to sell it. Hsing met them as they came to the city gates at dawn, for it was the very day stated in the dream, and he bought back the stone for two strings of cash.

※

For the rest of his long life Hsing kept the stone close to him, displayed in the inner room. In his eighty-seventh year he grew ill, and calling his son to him, he bade him bury the stone with him when he died. And so it was done.

Six months after Hsing's death, a pair of robbers broke into the burial vault and stole the stone, and the family was unable to recover it. Some weeks later, as his son was traveling with his servants, two men rushed out onto the road before them, bathed in sweat and looking wildly about. They confessed to having stolen the stone and asked the son to pray that his father's spirit would cease tormenting them.

Hsing's son brought the robbers before the local magistrate. They acknowledged their guilt and told him where the stone could be found. But upon seeing the stone, the magistrate also grew desirous of possessing it. He ordered his servants to take it and put it in his treasury.

But when the servants went to pick it up, the stone slipped from their hands and fell to the floor. To the astonishment of all, it shattered like glass into a hundred pieces. The magistrate had the thieves whipped and sent away. But Hsing's son gathered up the broken pieces and returned them to his father's grave.

The Taoist Priest
of Lao Shan

In our town there lived a man named Wang, who from his youth had been drawn to the teachings of Taoism. Hearing that on the mountain of Lao Shan were many Taoist priests who had attained immortality, he shouldered his pack and set off in search of them.

Near the top of the mountain, he came upon a secluded temple. Sitting there on a rush mat was a priest with long white hair and an expression of contentment on his face. Wang approached. He bowed to the priest and begged to be taught the secret wisdom of the Tao.

"I fear you are too delicate to endure the hardship of the way," replied the priest.

"Please allow me to try," pleaded Wang.

Toward evening, the other disciples of the priest gathered, and Wang was admitted to their number. The next morning at dawn, the priest called for him, gave him an ax, and told him to go out with the others to gather fire-wood. This went on day after day, dawn to dusk. At the end of a month, Wang's hands were badly blistered, his feet were swollen and sore, and he had secretly decided to return home.

﷼

One evening, when he got back from work, Wang found the master sitting drinking with two strangers. The sun had gone down and it was dark, but the lamps had not yet been brought in. The master took a pair of scissors and cut a circle from a piece of paper. He stuck it on the wall, and instantly it became a brilliant moon. By its light even a fine hair could be seen.

The disciples came crowding around to wait upon the company, but one of the guests said, "On a festive night such as this, we should all enjoy ourselves." He took up a kettle of wine from the table and bade them all take their fill.

Wang wondered how a single kettle could serve seven or eight of them. The others rushed around looking for cups and hurried to get in line before the wine was gone. But it was poured out freely, time and again, and they failed to empty the kettle, at which they were much astonished.

Soon the other guest said, "You have given us moon-light and wine, and yet still we drink alone. Let us call Chang-ngo, the Fairy of the Moon, to join us." Taking up a chopstick, he threw it into the moon. And behold, a lovely maiden stepped forth from the light. She was barely a foot high at first, but no sooner had she touched the ground than she grew to normal size. She had a slender waist and a long neck, and she danced the Red Skirt dance for them with grace. When she had finished, she entertained them with a song, and her voice was as clear and pure as a flute. Then she did a little pirouette, leapt up onto the table, and, before the startled eyes of all, was transformed again into a chopstick.

The three friends laughed heartily, and one said, "We are in a merry mood tonight. But I have almost had my fill of wine. Let us drink one parting glass together in the palace of the moon." So, without further ado, they took up their table and walked into the moon, where their silhouettes could be plainly seen.

In time the moon began to darken. The disciples ran to fetch lamps. And when they came back, there was only the master, seated alone in the dark. The remains of the wine were still on the table, and the circle of paper was still stuck to the wall.

"If you have all had enough to drink," said the priest, "you should get to bed, so as not to be late about your chores in the morning."

Wang was delighted at all he had seen that night, and the thought of returning home vanished from his mind.

❖

Another month passed by. Still Wang gathered firewood from dawn till dusk, and still the master had not begun to instruct him in the magical art of immortality. Finally he

32

could stand it no longer. He sought audience with the master, and when he came before him he said, "Sir, I have traveled hundreds of miles to receive instruction from you. Yet all day long, for months on end, all I have done is gather firewood. I am not accustomed to such a rigorous life. If you cannot show me the secret of immortality, perhaps there is some small feat you could teach me to satisfy my thirst for knowledge."

"I told you from the beginning you could not endure the hardship of discipleship," said the priest. "And now you have proven it. Tomorrow you must start for home."

"Sir, I have worked for you for many days. Is there not some skill you could teach me so that my time will not have been totally wasted?"

"What skill?" asked the master.

"Well, I have noticed," said Wang, "that wherever you walk, walls offer no impediment to your passage. If you could only show me how to do that, I would be satisfied."

The priest laughingly agreed. He taught Wang an incantation, which he had him recite until he had it by heart.

"Now," he said, "face that wall and go through."

Wang hesitated, walked forward a few steps, then stopped at the wall.

"Not so slow," said the priest. "Put your head down and run at it."

Wang stepped back, steeled himself, and ran at the wall at full tilt. This time it seemed to vanish before him, and turning around, he discovered he was outside the room. Delighted, he went back to express his thanks.

"Now, when you return home," said the master, "be wise in the use of this power, or the spell will not work." Then he gave Wang some money for his traveling expenses and sent him on his way.

❖

When Wang got back home, he bragged about his new Taoist friends and his general disdain for all walls. His wife would not believe his story, however, so he determined to prove it to her.

He stepped back several paces from the wall of the room, carefully recited the incantation the priest had taught him, then rushed full speed at the wall with his head down. He smacked his head hard against it and collapsed in a heap on the floor. His wife ran to pick him up and discovered he had a bump on his forehead the size of an egg. Despite herself, she burst out laughing, while Wang cursed the old priest for having tricked him.

Pianpian, the Leaf Fairy

Lu had lost both his parents as a child and had been taken in by his uncle Dahai, a civil servant in Fen District who loved him like a son. When he was fourteen, Lu fell in with bad company, ran away from home, and soon squandered all his money. Stricken with terrible boils that covered him from head to foot, he was reduced to begging by the road. People turned their faces when they saw him, and he grew afraid that he would die among strangers.

So he started back home, begging for food along the way. He walked fifteen to twenty miles a day and soon found himself at the border of Fen District. He was so ragged and filthy that he was ashamed to face his uncle. He lingered in a nearby neighborhood for the whole day. When dark fell, he made his way to a temple to seek shelter for the night.

But as he was walking along the road, he met a beautiful young woman. She asked him where he was going, and he told her all.

"I have abandoned the world and live alone in a cave in the mountains," she said. "I can offer you a bed for the night. You need have no fear of tigers or wolves."

Lu readily agreed to go with her. They went up into the mountains and came by and by to the mouth of a cave. A small stone bridge spanned a brook that ran by the entranceway. From within the cave came a light that brightened the darkness round about.

The young woman told Lu to take off his rags and bathe in the brook. "The water will begin to heal your boils," she said. "After you bathe you must sleep, and I will make something for you to wear."

The pain from the boils had lessened. Lu lay in bed and watched the girl as she took several large banana leaves and cut and sewed them into clothes. She laid them across the foot of the bed. "You can put these on tomorrow," she said, and she lay dawn in a bed across from him.

Come morning, the boils had been reduced to scabs. Lu arose, wondering how he should put on the leaf clothes she had made him. But when he picked them up, he found that they were fashioned out of fine green silk.

When it came time to eat, the girl gathered up a few dry leaves from the floor of the cave and set about baking them into a cake. She took up others and cut them into the shapes of a chicken and a fish, and cooked them. But when she brought them to the table and Lu tasted them, he found they were real. There was also a jug of wine from which they drank. And as it emptied, she topped it off with water, yet the quality of the wine remained unchanged.

In a few days all the scabs on his body had fallen away and Lu was completely healed. By then, all thought of returning home had been cast aside. He had fallen in love.

꩜

Day melted into day and month into month. Then one day there came a visitor to the cave, a young woman.

"Huacheng," cried the girl, running to embrace her. "How good it is to see you! It's been so long since you were last here. Tell me, was it the west wind, which blows so furiously today, that brought you? And where is your baby girl?"

"She has just fallen off to sleep," said the young woman. "And you, Pianpian, how have you been? It looks as if you've been having all the fun."

Pianpian introduced her to Lu, and the three sat down and drank wine together. All the while they were drinking, Huacheng kept looking at Lu. She, too, was very beautiful, and despite himself, he found he was attracted to her. At one point a piece of fruit he was peeling fell to the floor and as he bent to pick it up, his hand happened to brush against her foot. She gave him a knowing smile, and while she continued laughing and joking with Pianpian, she took Lu's hand in hers under the table. Lu felt a thrill of excitement go through him, and with his senses all awhirl, he chanced to look down and found himself covered not in silken robes but in dead leaves.

Horrified, he snatched his hand away and tried to calm himself, sitting as still as possible, and hoping that the two would not notice the change. By and by the clothes turned back to silk.

A short time later, Huacheng rose from the table. "I'd better go check on my baby," she said. "She may be crying for me."

"Yes," said Pianpian, "it's hard to keep one's mind on one's duties when one is attempting to seduce a stranger."

When she left, Lu was afraid that Pianpian would scold him, but she said nothing further of the matter.

Soon, the wind grew cold, the green leaves dried and withered, and winter came. The girl fashioned clothes for Lu from the fallen leaves, but he was still freezing. So she caught up armfuls of the cloudy fog that floated past the entrance to the cave and wove it into a garment as soft as fur and as light as feathers for him.

⁂

The following year Pianpian gave birth to a son, a good-looking boy and very bright. Lu passed his time playing with the child, but he found himself thinking frequently of home. More than once he asked Pianpian to go back with him.

"I cannot do that," she would say, "but you may go yourself."

He put it off. Time went by, and the child grew. Pianpian taught the boy to read by scratching characters on leaves. He learned everything with extraordinary ease. When he grew older, his parents discussed with Huacheng the possibility of an engagement between their two children. Huacheng agreed, and when the two were of a marriageable age, she brought her daughter all decked in jewels to them. Amid great feasting, the couple were wed. They settled into a neighboring cave.

⋇

One day Pianpian said to Lu, "Our son belongs to the ways of the world, not to those of the fairies. Take him back home with his bride to your uncle. He will rise to a high rank and win honor."

It was hard for the newlyweds to leave home. Tears ran down their faces, but their mothers comforted them and assured them they would one day return. Then Pianpian cut out the shape of a mule from leaves, and the three of them rode off to Lu's home.

His uncle Dahai had grown old and retired from office. He had long assumed his nephew was dead. Now, when Lu appeared unexpectedly and presented the old man not only with a grandnephew but with a beautiful grandniece, he was as overjoyed as if he had come upon a priceless treasure.

But when the three travelers crossed the threshold of the house, their fine clothes turned to withered leaves and they were forced to find new clothes to cover themselves. Time passed and they all prospered.

Some years later, Lu and his son rode into the mountains to look for Pianpian. A tangle of yellow leaves barred the entrance to the cave, and fog choked the path. With tears in their eyes, they returned home.

Past Lives

A certain Mr. Lin claimed he could remember his previous lives. One day he was prevailed upon to recount his remarkable story, and this is what he said:

"I came in the beginning from a good family, but led a dissolute life, and died at the age of sixty-two. When I was brought before the king of Purgatory, he invited me to sit down and offered me a cup of tea. I noticed that the tea in his cup was clear, while that in mine was murky; and the thought came to me that this was the potion given to all the spirits of the dead to make them oblivious of the past. So while the king was looking the other way, I emptied the cup on the ground and pretended to have drunk it up.

"The record of my good and evil deeds was brought before the king. When he had examined it, he flew into a rage and ordered the attendant demons to drag me off and send me back to Earth as a horse. The devils seized and bound me and carried me off to a house. But the doorsill was so high that I could not step over it. And all the while I was trying, the demons were lashing me from behind, causing me such pain that at last I lunged over the doorsill . . .

". . . And found myself lying on the floor of a stable.

"'The mare has got a nice colt,' I heard a man say. Yet while I was perfectly aware of all that was going on about me, I could not speak. A great hunger came upon me then, and I was glad to be suckled by the mare. By the end of five years, I had grown into a fine strong horse. But I was always terribly afraid of the whip, and would bolt at the very sight of one.

"My master was kindly; he always rode me with a saddlecloth and was happy to canter along at a quiet pace. But the servants were cruel and would ride me bareback, digging their heels into my sides to make me go faster. Finally, I could bear it no longer. I refused all food and, in three days, died.

⚜

"I came again before the king of Purgatory, who was enraged that I had thereby shirked working out my time, and ordered that I go back to Earth as a dog. When I refused to move, the demons came with their whips and lashed me, until I ran off into the open country to escape them. Coming at length to a cliff, I flung myself off, hoping to end it all. But as I struck the ground . . .

". . . I found myself among a litter of puppies, whose mother proceeded to lick and suckle me along with the others. I continued in this puppy form for some time, unhappy and ill-used. One day my master took the whip to me. I bit him on the leg and drew blood; whereupon, he ordered me destroyed.

"Again I was brought before the king of Purgatory, who was so upset at my behavior that he condemned me to return to Earth a snake. He had me shut inside a dark room, where I could see nothing. I managed somehow to climb the wall and bore a hole in the roof, through which I made my escape . . .

". . . Only to find myself a snake, slithering from its hole. This time I determined to do ill to no living thing. And so I passed my life in peace, feeding on berries and such, remembering not to take my own life or, by injuring another, to cause him to take it, but longing only and always for the day of my release.

"One day, as I lay sleeping on the grass, I heard the noise of an approaching cart, and on trying to get out of its path, I was run over by the wheel and cut in two.

"The king was amazed to see me again so soon. But upon hearing my story, he took pity on me and pardoned me, allowing that I might be born again as a human being at the appointed hour."

❧

So ends the strange story of Mr. Lin. It was said that he could speak as soon as he came into the world. And his memory was such that if he read a thing but once, he could remember it perfectly. He took his master's degree in the year 1621, and throughout his long life, he never tired of telling people to wear saddlecloths upon their horses and to spare the whip.

Paper Robes

A certain old man and his son kept a roadside inn in a village some miles from the district city, where travelers might pass the night. One evening, as it was growing dark, four strangers came knocking and asked for a night's lodging.

"I fear that every bed is taken," apologized the innkeeper.

"It is too late for us to go on," said one of the travelers. "Surely there is something."

After a long pause, the innkeeper said, "Yes, there may be something that will suit you – if you are not too particular."

"Anything will do," they assured him.

The sad truth was that the innkeeper's daughter-in-law had just died, and her body was laid out in a room in the women's quarters, while his son was off to buy a coffin. It was there the innkeeper led them.

He placed the lamp upon the table. At the far end of the room lay the corpse, dressed in the traditional paper robes. At the near end lay four sleeping mats. The travelers were bone tired, and without further ado, laid themselves down and were soon snoring. All save one, who had not yet dozed off when he heard a creaking of the bier at the far end of the room where the corpse was laid.

He opened his eyes and watched in terror as the dead girl stirred, with a rustling of the paper robes. She sat up and in an instant slipped to the floor and began crossing the room toward them. She had a silken kerchief tied about her head, and her face was the color of old parchment.

She reached the mats and, one by one, bent down and blew upon the faces of the sleepers. The one who was still awake drew the covers up over his head, held his breath, and waited. He sensed her stooping over him, felt the chill ripple of the sheets against his face as she breathed upon him, heard the faint rustle of the paper robes as she crossed the room and climbed back upon the bier.

At length he opened his eyes a crack. The girl was lying there as before. Careful to make no noise, he stretched out his foot and gently prodded each of his companions in turn, but all lay still as stone. He determined to make his escape, but hardly had he moved, when again he heard the creak of the bier. He darted back under the bedclothes, and again the dead girl came and breathed upon him several times, then finally crossed back to her bier and lay down again, with a light rustle of the paper robes.

Immediately the man reached out his hand, found his trousers, and slid quickly into them; then he bounded from the room as fast as his legs would carry him. The corpse leapt up as well. He drew back the bolt on the door of the women's quarters and ran out shrieking into the night, with the dead girl close upon his heels.

No one seemed to hear his cries. He was afraid to knock on the door of the inn lest they should not open it in time. So he kept running, making for the road to the city.

Not far along the road he came upon a monastery, and hearing the chanting of the monks within, he headed for the gate and banged upon it with all his might.

"Let me in!" he cried. "Let me in."

But the monk inside thought he was a madman, and would not open the gate.

By now the corpse was close behind, and as he could think of nothing else to do, he dashed behind a tree. There he sheltered himself, dodging to the right then the left, keeping always beyond the girl's reach, until finally, in her fury, she made a mad rush forward, reaching both arms round the tree in an effort to snare her victim. But the traveler fell backwards and escaped, while the corpse remained fixed in a rigid embrace of the tree.

Finally, the monk who had been listening from inside the gate, hearing no sound for some time, went out to investigate, and found the traveler lying on the ground in a faint. He carried him into the monastery, where, by morning, he had recovered sufficiently to take a little broth. Then the traveler told the monks his tale, and in the uncertain light of dawn, they ventured out and found the corpse still fixed to the tree.

They sent for the magistrate. He ordered the body removed. But try though they might they could not readily loose her, for her fingers had driven into the bark deeper than the nails. Finally they freed her, and a messenger was sent to the inn, which was all in a turmoil over the three travelers found dead in their beds.

The old innkeeper sent his servants to carry back the body of his daughter-in-law. And the surviving traveler petitioned the magistrate to give him something that he might show to his townsmen when he returned home, that suspicion might not fall upon him.

"For four of us left, and only one returns."

So the magistrate gave him a letter certifying the strange events told here, and sent the man on his way.

Jen Shui, the Gambler

Jen Chien-shih was a dealer in rugs and furs. One day he scraped together all the money he had saved and set off for the capital to sell his wares. On the way he met a man whose name was Shen Chu-ting. The two quickly became friends and swore to stand by one another through thick and thin. Together they journeyed to the capital, where Jen soon prospered in his affairs.

However, as chance would have it, he fell ill. For ten days his friend nursed him faithfully, but he continued to decline. Finally he said to Shen: "My family is very poor. Eight mouths depend upon me. And now I am about to die on strange soil, far from home. I have no one here I can trust but you, my friend. In my bag you will find more than two hundred ounces of silver. Take half of it, pay for my funeral expenses, and put the balance toward your return journey; when you get back, give the other

49

half to my family, and ask that they have my coffin carried back to be laid alongside my ancestors. However, should you decide to carry my body back yourself, these expenses need not be incurred." Then, propped up on a pillow, he wrote a letter, which he handed to Shen. That evening he died.

Shen put five or six ounces of silver toward a cheap coffin for his friend. When the landlord kept pressing him to take away the body, he said he would go and look for a temple where he could temporarily leave it. Instead, he ran off with the rest of Jen's money and never returned.

❧

A year went by before Jen's family discovered what had happened to him. His son Shui was seventeen at the time and was studying under a tutor. But now he laid his books aside and said he would go in search of his father's body. His mother said he was too young, but he begged her, saying he would sooner die than stay at home now. So she pawned some of their possessions and raised enough money to start him on his way. An old servant went with him. Six months later, they returned with Jen's remains and performed the burial ceremonies.

They were left destitute. But Shui was a clever fellow, and when the period of mourning was at an end, he completed his studies and graduated. His mother wanted him to go on and take a teaching degree, but the truth was, he was somewhat of a wild lad and felt his fortune lay another way. He had a fondness for gambling and did well at it, and though his mother cautioned him against it, all her warnings were in vain.

It happened that an uncle of his, named Chang, was about to go to the capital to trade his merchandise. He asked Shui to come along and offered to pay his expenses. Shui was only too happy to accept. They sailed together to Lin-ching, where they anchored their boat outside the Custom House. There were a great number of other boats gathered there, a forest of masts.

It was late, but with the noise of the water and the clamor of voices from the boats, sleep was impossible. Finally, things began to quiet down, and then, separating itself from the other sounds, came the clear rattle of dice from a neighboring boat. This was music to Shui's ears and he itched to join in the game. But his mother's warnings returned to him. Three times he rose and loosed his purse strings; three times he drew them closed and returned to bed. Finally the temptation was too much for him. He listened to be sure that his uncle was asleep, then got up quietly with his money and crossed over into the boat from which the sounds came.

There were two men gambling there for high stakes. Shui put his string of cash on the table and asked if he could join in. The others readily agreed, and they started to play. Immediately Shui began to win, and the stakes grew higher and higher as the others tried to recoup their losses. The game was in full swing, when suddenly another man walked in. He stood for a long while watching, then asked the boat keeper if he could change a piece of silver so that he might join in the game. The boat keeper agreed, and the stranger sat down with them.

Meanwhile, Shui's uncle, waking up in the middle of the night and finding his nephew gone, heard the noise of dice from the neighboring boat and guessed immediately where he was. He crossed over to the boat with the intention of bringing him back. Finding that Shui was winning heavily, however, he said nothing, but carried off a portion of the winnings to their boat. He made several trips, but still left Shui a large sum to go on with.

By and by the others had lost all their money and there was nothing left on the boat. The stranger who had come in last proposed that they play for lumps of silver, but Shui said he never played for such high stakes. The stranger grew a little testy at this, and Shui's uncle urged his nephew to return to their boat. But the boat keeper, eager for his commission, took all the silver the stranger had, and going from boat to boat, managed to borrow enough cash to exchange for it.

The game went on, the stakes increased, and soon all the money had again gone to Shui. By now day was dawning and the Custom House was about to open, so Shui gathered up his winnings and went back to his own boat.

In the clear light of day, the keeper of the gambling boat discovered that the lumps of silver he had exchanged for cash were nothing more than worthless rocks. He rushed off in a great state of alarm to Shui's boat, told him what had happened, and demanded that Shui make good his losses. But it chanced that, during the course of their conversation, he learned Shui's name and where he had come from, and immediately he realized that this was the son of his former traveling companion, Jen Chien-shih. He hung his head and slunk away in shame, for he was none other than the scoundrel Shen Chu-ting.

Then Shui realized that the stranger on the boat had in fact been the spirit of his father, taken human form to help his son avenge the evil done to him. Shui decided to pursue the scoundrel no further, but taking his winnings from that night, he went into partnership with his uncle. They traveled north together, and by the end of the year, his capital had increased fivefold. By means of his wealth, he purchased a position of high standing. His family prospered and soon he was the richest man in that part of the country.

The Invisible Priest

Mr. Han, a gentleman from a good family, was on friendly terms with a certain Taoist priest and magician named Tan. This Tan was famous for his ability, when sitting among company, to become invisible. Han was anxious to learn this art, but Tan steadfastly refused to teach it to him.

"It is not simply because I wish to keep the secret to myself," he explained. "It is a matter of principle. To teach one such as yourself would be one thing, but what if the knowledge were to fall into the hands of others who might use it to plunder their neighbors?"

Finding all his efforts in vain, Han flew into a passion and secretly arranged with his servants to give the priest a sound thrashing. But first, to prevent him escaping by becoming invisible, he had the floors sprinkled with a fine ash-dust so that his footsteps would be seen, and the servants could strike just above them.

The unsuspecting Tan walked into the trap. Immediately the servants set upon him and began beating him with leather thongs. And though he quickly grew invisible, his footprints betrayed his whereabouts and the servants went on striking him. Finally he managed to make his escape.

❧

Some days later he appeared at Han's door, carrying his few belongings. He announced to the servants that he had decided to leave, but before he went he intended to give them all a feast in thanks for the many things that they had done for him. Reaching into his wide sleeves, he brought out a quantity of delicious meats and wines, which he spread upon the table. He begged them to sit down and enjoy themselves. One by one the servants grew drunk, and Tan plucked them up and tucked them away in his sleeve.

When Han heard what had happened, he came running and demanded to know what had become of his servants.

"Observe," said Tan, and taking from his robe a piece of chalk, he began to draw upon the wall a city, replete with walls and towers. When he was done, he knocked at the gate with his hand, and it was instantly thrown open. He put his bundle of belongings inside it, then stepped through the gateway himself. He turned and waved good-bye to Mr. Han, who stood dumbfounded while the gate of the city closed, and priest and servants and all vanished into the wall.

The Man Who Was
Changed into a Crow

Mr. Yu came from a poor family in Hu-nan. One day he was returning home after having failed his examinations in the city. He had run out of money, but was too ashamed to beg. Feeling weak from hunger, he stopped to rest awhile in the temple of Wu Wang, the guardian spirit of the crows.

Yu had poured out his sorrows at the feet of the god and was about to lie down to rest on the porch of the temple, when he was approached by a young man, who ushered him into the presence of Wu Wang himself. The young man went down on his knees before the god and said: "Your Majesty, there is a vacancy among the black robes. Perhaps the appointment could be bestowed upon this man."

The god agreed, and Yu was presented with a suit of black clothes. He put them on and was immediately changed into a crow. He took to the air and joined a flock of other crows, settling with them on the masts of the boats that traveled down the river that ran past the temple. Imitating them, he soon learned to fly down and catch the little cakes and pieces of meat that the boatmen and their passengers threw to them to secure favorable passage on their journey.

Soon he was no longer hungry, and found himself quite satisfied with his change of state. Time passed, and the god, taking pity on Yu's solitary life, sent him a mate named Chu-ch'ing. She warned him to be wary of hunters while he searched for food, but Yu failed to heed her advice and was shot in the breast by a soldier with a crossbow. Chu-ch'ing flew away with Yu in her beak, and did all she could for him, but the wound was severe, and by day's end he was dead . . .

. . . At which moment he woke up as if from a dream and found himself lying in the temple. The people of the temple had found him, to all appearances, dead, and not knowing how he had died and discovering the body still warm, had set someone to watch over him. It was then he had revived. He told them his strange tale, and collecting money between them, they sent him on home.

❧

Three years passed, and one day Yu, having finally succeeded in obtaining his master's degree, passed by the temple again on his way home. He sacrificed a sheep as a feast for the crows. And when they flew down he prayed: "If Chu-ch'ing is among you, let her remain."

But when they had eaten their fill, all the birds flew off.

That night, as he sat inside his boat on the river, Yu heard a noise like the beating of wings. Suddenly, standing before him was a beautiful young woman of about twenty years of age.

"Have you been well since we parted?" she asked.

But he said he did not know her.

"Do you not remember your Chu-ch'ing?" she asked.

At this Yu was overjoyed and asked her how she had come to him.

"I am now a spirit of the Han River," she said, "and seldom come back to my old home. But because you have called, I have come again to see you."

Yu asked her to return home with him, but she said she could not, for she must return to her river. They sat talking together, husband and wife reunited, until late into the night.

When he awoke in the morning, Yu found he was no longer in his boat on the river, but in a large room where two candles were burning by the bed. Greatly astonished, he rose up and asked where he was.

"You are at my home on the Han River," said Chu-ch'ing. "Stay with me. You have no need to go south again."

"But what of my servants? And what of the boat that is waiting for me?"

But she told him she had taken care of everything.

As it grew lighter, serving women came to them with wine, and husband and wife sat down to drink together. And so time passed, day into day, week into week, as smoothly as the water that flowed past their house on the Han River.

Yet, by and by, thoughts of home came to him again. And one day he said to Chu-ch'ing: "If I stay here longer, my family will forget me." And again he pleaded with her to return with him.

"That I cannot do," she said. "And besides, you have a wife at home already. Where would you put me? It is better that I stay here and you visit me as a second family."

"But I will be so far away that I shall seldom see you," he said.

At this Chu-ch'ing brought out a folded black suit and said: "Here are your old clothes. Whenever you wish to see me, put them on and come to me." She then prepared a parting feast for him, at which he grew quite tipsy.

When he awoke, he found himself on board his old boat on the river by the temple. Folded by his side was the black suit and an embroidered belt stuffed full of gold. He started homeward, his servants with him, and when their journey ended, he paid the boatmen handsomely.

※

Months passed and Yu found his thoughts turning more and more to Chu-ch'ing, so one day he took out the suit of black and put it on. Immediately feathers grew over his flesh and wings sprang from his ribs. He took to the air and, in no time at all, found himself over the Han River. On a tiny island there he spied a solitary house and flew down to it.

The servants had seen him coming. And when he landed, Chu-ch'ing was there to meet him. She bade the servants set him free from his feathers, and together they went into the house.

"You have come at a happy moment," she said, and in three days she gave birth to a boy, whom they called Han-ch'an, which means 'born on the Han River.' The river spirits came to congratulate them and brought many wonderful presents.

Soon Yu returned home to the south, but after this he came back often to the Han River. The boy grew strong and healthy and was the apple of his father's eye.

Now, Yu's first wife had no children, and she was anxious to see Han-ch'an. Yu told this to Chu-ch'ing and she immediately packed up a box and sent the boy back with his father, on the understanding that he would be returned to her in three months.

But Yu's first wife grew as fond of the boy as if he had been her own, and nine months passed without her being able to part with him.

Then one day Han-ch'an was taken violently ill, and died that very night. The wife was so distraught that, for a time, Yu thought that she too might die. He put on his black suit and flew to Chu-ch'ing with the tragic news.

But when he arrived, great was his surprise to find the boy there in his old bed, perfectly well. He asked Chu-ch'ing to explain what it all meant.

"Why," she said, "the term of his visit had long passed, and I wanted my boy back; so I sent for him."

Yu explained how attached his first wife had grown to the boy. But Chu-ch'ing said she must wait until there was another child, and then she would send the boy to her. Some time later she had twins, a boy and a girl, whereupon she sent Han-ch'an back to the south with his father.

⁂

At twelve years of age, Han-ch'an took his bachelor's degree. When he was old enough to marry, his mother, thinking there was no girl among mortals suited for her son, sent for him again and found him a wife, who like herself was the daughter of a spirit.

In the fullness of time, Yu's first wife died. The three children went to mourn her. Han-ch'an remained in Hunan after the funeral, but the twins and their father returned to the north, and lived happily together with Chu-ch'ing in the house on the Han River.

The Glass Eyes

One day Tang's uncle took him to a temple to see the theatrical performances. Tang was a clever boy, afraid of nothing and nobody; and when he saw one of the clay images in the vestibule staring at him with its great glass eyes, the temptation was too much. When no one was watching, he reached up and plucked them out and carried them off in his pocket.

No sooner had they reached home than Tang's uncle was inexplicably struck ill. He remained speechless for several days. Then, suddenly one morning, he sprang up in the bed and cried out in a voice like thunder: "Why did you gouge out my eyes?" Several times he shouted the question, his eyes shut like one asleep.

The family had no idea what to make of it all, until little Tang came forward and confessed what he had done. Immediately the family gathered about the possessed man and beseeched him, saying, "A mere child, unconscious of the wickedness of the deed, has snatched away your sacred eyes. They shall reverently be replaced."

Thereupon, the uncle's lips parted, and the voice said, "In that case, I shall depart."

Hardly were the words spoken than the uncle fell into a faint and remained that way for some time. When at length he recovered, the family asked him about the things he had said, but the man had no memory of it.

As for the glass eyes, they were carried back that same day to the temple, where Tang reached up and returned them to the empty sockets of the clay statue.

The Two Friends

When Chen was sixteen, he was sent to a day school in a Buddhist temple. There were a large number of other students there, among them a boy named Chu, who said he came from Shan-tung. Chu was a hardworking student, who never seemed to be idle; and whereas all the other students went home at the end of each day, he slept in the empty schoolroom and never went home at all. The two boys soon became friends, and one day Chen asked him why he never went home.

"Well," said Chu, "my parents are very poor and can barely afford to send me to school at all. So by staying here and working half the night, I am able to finish in two days what the other students finish in three. And so I shall graduate sooner."

Chen suggested that he could bring his sleeping mat to the school as well, and in that way they could study together. Chu replied that the teaching they were receiving at the temple was not that good anyway. And if they were to study together, they would do better to place themselves in the care of a certain old scholar named Lu. Chen readily agreed, and so the two set off to see Mr. Lu.

Now, this Mr. Lu was a writer of considerable merit, but as he found himself short of money, he was more than pleased to take on the two as students. He was much taken with Chu, who proved to be an excellent scholar. He allowed the boy to board with him, while Chen returned each evening to his parents' home.

And so things went for some time, until Chu asked if he might take a leave of absence. He left that night. At the end of two weeks, they had still not heard from him. Then one day Chen happened to visit the Tien-ning temple, and there under one of the verandas he saw his friend chopping wood to be used for lucifer matches. He approached him, and the two exchanged greetings.

"But why have you given up your studies?" Chen asked.

Chu took him aside. "I have not enough money to pay Mr. Lu," he explained. "And so I am working half a month to scrape together enough cash to pay next month's schooling."

On hearing this, Chen said to him, "Come back with me and I will take care of the payment." Chu finally agreed, on condition that Chen keep the arrangement secret.

Now, Chen's father was a wealthy trader, and it was from his till that Chen took the money for his friend's schooling. One day his father caught him in the act, and he was forced to confess everything. His father called him a fool and refused to let him continue his studies.

Chu was distraught. He blamed himself for what had happened, and told Mr. Lu that, along with his friend Chen, he too must quit his studies. But when old Mr. Lu learned why, he gave Chu the money to return to Chen's father, and he kept the boy on as his student, treating him like a son.

❧

Time passed, and though the two no longer studied together, Chen made a point of keeping up their friendship. Some time later, Chen's father died and the boy went back to study with his friend again, under Mr. Lu. He had fallen far behind Chu now in his studies, and the graduate examinations were to begin shortly – a difficult ordeal that went on for nine days. Mr. Lu suggested that Chen take Chu as his tutor, which he did, inviting his friend to share his house with him. Still, he was convinced that he would not get through the exams. But Chu told him to leave matters in his hands and not to worry.

On the day before the exams, Chu introduced Chen to his cousin Liu, who was having a party that day. He suggested that Chen go with him and enjoy himself before the ordeal of the exams. They were on their way out the door when suddenly Chu pulled Chen back into him from behind. Chen would have fallen to the ground had the cousin not put out his hand and pulled him up, looking at him intently all the while.

Off they went to Liu's house. There were a great many people gathered in the garden and lounging on the grass, which sloped down to a little stream. Chen and Liu took tea together and drank wine under a willow tree. There was a small painted boat drawn up on the shore nearby, and before long they had boarded it and were drifting in the stream.

Liu called to his servant and bade him go and ask Miss Li, a famous singer who was among the guests, if she would favor them with a song. At length Miss Li appeared. Chen, who had met her before, exchanged warm greetings with her.

"Will you sing for us?" asked Liu.

To their surprise, the girl began to sing a funeral dirge. It was heartfelt and moving, but hardly appropriate for a party. Chen asked her if she might sing them a love song instead: "Perhaps the song of the Huan-sha River, which I heard you sing once before."

With a forced smile, the girl stopped her dirge and began to sing the love song, while the boat drifted near shore.

Soon it was evening, and Liu offered to take Chen back home. They left the boat on the bank and walked along a walled path that bordered the garden. Chen noticed that a great many verses had been written on the wall there, and he stopped and added one of his own.

❧

He arrived back home in something of a daze. Alone in the house, he sat in the dark and dreamt of the girl who had sung the love song to him. By and by the servants came in with someone whom he took to be Chu, though he could not see his face in the dark. He rose to greet him, but as the figure approached, he realized it was not Chu. And in the next instant the figure fell against him heavily and collapsed onto the ground.

"Master's fainted," cried the servants. And as they rushed forward and picked him up, Chen realized that the stranger who had fallen was, in fact, himself. And the figure standing where he had stood one instant before was Chu. He sent the servants away.

"Don't be alarmed," said Chu. "I am a disembodied spirit. My time for reappearing on Earth is long overdue, but I could not forget your kindness to me, so I have stayed that I might assist you in your heart's desire. Nine days have drifted past while you sat in your boat on the stream. Before you left, when I pulled you from behind, I exchanged your form for mine, and now I have returned it to you. In the meantime, I have taken the exams in your stead. I assure you, you will do well. And now, my friend, I must leave."

"But where will you go?"

"I return to the land of spirits and await the appointed hour to be reborn. I have a cousin who is a clerk in purgatory. Perhaps, through his influence, I can arrange to be reborn into old Mr. Lu's family."

He held out his palms and asked Chen to write the name *Chu* on each. Then the two friends parted, with Chu promising they would meet again.

Chen wiped away his tears as he saw his friend to the door. There was a man there waiting for Chu, and as he came out the door the man laid a hand on his head and pressed down until Chu was perfectly flat. Then the man popped him in a sack and carried him off.

The following day Chen set off to call on Miss Li, the singer. But when he arrived at her house, he was told that she had been dead for some days. He walked on to Liu's house, but found it empty and the garden overgrown. On the walls that flanked the path he saw faint traces of ancient verses, all but indecipherable now. He knew then that the verses and those who had written them were all inhabitants of the other world.

It was not long before the examination list came out. To his great joy, Chen found his name among the successful candidates. Immediately he went off to tell his old teacher, Mr. Lu.

Now it so happened that Mr. Lu's wife, who was past fifty and had had no children for ten years, had just given birth to a baby boy, who had been born with both fists doubled up so that no one could open them. Chen begged to see the child, and was brought to the room where it lay. No sooner did the baby set eyes on him than both its fists opened instantly. There on the palms was written the name *Chu*.

The Talking Eye Pupils

At Chang-on there lived a scholar named Fang Tung. He was not without talent, but he fancied himself something of a ladies' man, and thought nothing of following and making advances to any woman he happened to meet.

The day before the spring festival called Clear Weather, he was walking outside the city when he caught sight of a small carriage with a red screen and an embroidered awning, followed by a number of waiting maids riding on horseback. One of them was quite pretty, so he worked his way a little closer to get a better look. It happened that the carriage screen was partly open, and he caught a glimpse inside of the most beautiful creature he had ever seen. She was about sixteen, exquisitely dressed, and lovely beyond words. He could not keep his eyes off her.

Fang followed the carriage for several miles, going now before, now behind. Presently he heard the girl call to one of her waiting maids. When the maid came alongside the carriage, the girl said, "Please let down the screen. I am tired of this rude fellow staring at me so."

The maid let down the screen, then turning angrily to Fang, she said, "This is the bride of the Seventh Prince of the City of the Immortals returning home to visit her parents, and not some common farm girl that the likes of you should be ogling." And taking up a handful of dust, she flung it in his face, momentarily blinding him. He rubbed his eyes, and when his vision cleared, he found that the carriage and the horses had vanished!

⽒

Unnerved by the whole business, he went home. There was still something wrong with his eyes, so he sent for the doctor, who found that a thin layer of film had grown over the pupils. By morning the film had thickened, and his eyes would not stop watering. The film kept on growing and, in a few days, it was as thick as a coin. No medicine was of any use. Sightless, Fang gave himself up to despair.

Then the thought of repentance entered his mind. He had heard somewhere that reciting the *Kuang-ming* sutra (The Book of Clear Light) could relieve misery. So he obtained a copy and hired someone to teach it to him.

Time passed; he grew more settled in his mind. He would spend the whole day sitting utterly still, praying his beads. By the end of a year, he had come to a state of perfect calm. It was then he first heard a small voice, no louder than the buzzing of a fly, calling out from his left eye, "It's horribly dark in here."

To this a voice replied from his right eye, saying, "Let's go out for a walk and cheer ourselves up a little."

Then he felt a wriggling in his nose, as though something was creeping out his nostrils. A while later, he felt it again, this time going the other way. Soon after, a voice from one eye said, "It's been a long while since I've seen the garden. What a pity all the epidendrums are dead."

Fang had been a great admirer of epidendrums. He had filled his garden with them, and would tend and water them himself, but since his blindness he had taken no thought of them. He called his wife to him now and asked her why she had let his epidendrums die. She asked how he knew they were dead, and when he told her, she went to look, and indeed they *were* dead.

Astonished at this, the wife decided to hide herself secretly in the room and see what she would see. In a little while, she watched two tiny people, no bigger than a bean, come out of her husband's nose and fly out the door, where she lost sight of them. A little later, they came back and flew up to his face, like bees seeking the entrance to their nest.

This went on for days, then Fang suddenly heard the voice from his left eye say, "This roundabout road is not at all convenient for coming and going. We would be much better off making a door."

"It wouldn't be an easy job," answered the voice from his right eye. "The wall is very thick here."

"I'll see what I can do with mine," said the left. "It could serve for the two of us."

And straightaway Fang felt a sharp pain in his left eye, as though something was being split apart. And behold, suddenly he could see the table and chairs, and all the rest of the things in the room. He ran to tell his wife. She examined his eye and found a crack in the film that covered it. Through it she could see the black pupil peering out. The eyeball itself looked like a split peppercorn.

By the following morning, the film had totally disappeared from that eye. The other eye remained as it was. But close examination of the good eye revealed the most remarkable thing. It appeared to contain two pupils, as if the pupils of both eyes had taken up residence in the one.

Fang remained blind in one eye, but the sight in the other was better than that of the two together. From that time on, he amended his former behavior and acquired a reputation as a virtuous man.

Theft of the Peach

When I was a little boy, I went to the city one day with a friend to see the Spring Festival. It was the custom on the day before the festival began for all the merchants to parade through the streets with banners and drums to the judge's residence. They called it "Bringing in the spring."

Caught up in the crowd, we were swept along to the courtyard of the judge's house, where all the city officials sat in their crimson robes, ranged in two rows on a dais. I was too young to care much about them; I was far more interested in the milling of the crowd and the sound of the drums.

Suddenly, in the midst of all this, a man, leading a boy of about my age, parted from the crowd and came up to where the officials were sitting. He was carrying a pole on his shoulder, and he and the boy carried a large wooden box between them. He spoke briefly to the officials, who seemed pleased with what he had to say. Then an attendant came forward and announced to the crowd that the man was going to perform.

"What would you like to see?" the man asked the officials.

"What can you do best?" they asked him in return.

"I can invert the order of nature," he replied.

Again there was some talk among the officials, and one of them said, "Can you produce some peaches for us, then?" It was far from the season for peaches. There was still a dusting of snow on the ground in places.

"That would be very hard," replied the performer. But his son reminded him of his promise, and after a few moments' thought, the man said, "I have it. We clearly can't get peaches here, but perhaps there are some in heaven. For there, on the shores of Gem Lake, the peach tree of the gods grows, and they say whoever eats of that fruit will never die."

"But how are we to get up there, Father?" asked the boy.

"Never fear. I have a way," said the man, and, opening his box, he removed a long coil of rope. He took one end and hurled it high into the air, where it stayed as if it had been caught by something. Slowly he began paying out the length of the rope. Up and up it went until the top of it disappeared among the clouds and he was left holding the other end.

He called to his son. "I'm too heavy to climb the rope," he said. "You must go."

"But the rope is too thin to carry me to such a height," said the boy. "I will fall down and be killed."

"But we have promised," said the father. "And if you do obtain the peaches, we shall no doubt be richly rewarded by these fine gentlemen, and I will set aside the money to get you a wife."

The boy took the end of the rope from him and scrambled up it as quickly as a spider scooting up its thread. Soon he had gone so high he was lost to sight.

The minutes passed. Suddenly, down fell a peach as big as a basin. The father, delighted, handed it to the officials. They were still debating whether it was real or not, when down plunged the rope in a heap.

"Oh, no, someone has cut the rope," cried the father. "What will my boy do now?"

The minutes passed, then another object fell at the man's feet with a thud. He picked it up. It was the boy's head! A cry of horror rose up from the crowd.

"Ah," wailed the father, "the gardener of the gods has caught my son, and now he is dead."

Down came the arms, then the legs, then the body of the boy. The father gathered them up and put them all in the box.

"This was my only son," said the father, "and for the sake of a peach, he is dead. I must arrange to bury him now. Pray help me pay the funeral expenses, and I will be ever grateful to you."

The officials, who had witnessed the whole horrific scene, collected among themselves a goodly sum of money for him. When the father had been given the money, he turned and rapped on the box, saying, "Son, come out and thank the gentlemen for their generosity."

There came a knock in reply from within the box. Then up flew the lid, and out popped the boy. A cry of amazement went up from the crowd as he bowed before them.

❧

Many years have gone by since that day, but I have never forgotten the terror and wonder I felt in witnessing that incredible illusion.

The Assistant to
the Thunder God

Yao Yun-hao and Shia Ping-tse had grown up in the same village, studied under the same tutor, and become the best of friends. Shia was naturally brilliant. Yao looked up to him, and Shia helped him with his studies, so that Yao too made considerable progress. There were great expectations of Shia, but when it came time for him to take the official examinations, he failed repeatedly. By and by, he grew sick and died.

Shia's family was so poor that they could not afford to pay the funeral expenses. Yao came forward and took them upon himself. He brought his friend's widow and children under his roof, and shared all that he and his own family had with them. His reputation for goodness grew, but his property diminished and he was soon in desperate straits.

"Where one as talented as Shia has failed, how can I expect to succeed? If I keep to my present course, I will end up dying like a dog in a ditch. I must give up book-learning and turn my hand to something more profitable."

So he took to trade, and within six months, had begun to see a little profit.

❧

One day, Yao happened to be staying at an inn in Nanking, when a huge fellow walked in and sat down at a neighboring table. He looked pale and heavyhearted. Yao asked him if he was hungry, but it was like talking to the wall. He pushed a plate of food in front of the stranger. The big fellow plunged into it and in no time it was gone. Yao ordered another plateful, and the stranger made short work of that as well. Then he told the innkeeper to bring them a shoulder of pork and a platter of steamed dumplings. The stranger downed enough to feed half a dozen people.

When he had had his fill, he turned to Yao and said, "I thank you, my friend. It's been three years since I've had such a meal."

"How could such an imposing fellow as yourself have fallen on such hard times?" asked Yao.

"The judgements of heaven are not to be questioned," replied the stranger.

Yao asked him where he lived.

"On land I have no home; on water, no boat. At dawn I am in a village; at dusk I am in a city."

Yao began to pack up his things, preparing to move on. But the stranger seemed reluctant to let him go.

"You have shown kindness to me," he said. "I cannot

let you wander off alone, for you are in grave danger." He would say no more. So off they went together.

While they were on their way, Yao offered his companion some food, but he refused, saying he ate only a few times a year. At this, Yao marveled more than ever.

⁂

The following day they were crossing a wide river, when suddenly a storm came up and capsized their boat and all their belongings with it. Yao and his companion were thrown into the river as well. Instantly the storm abated, and the stranger took Yao on his back and carried him to a nearby boat. Then he plunged into the water and brought up the lost boat, put Yao into it, and told him to wait there quietly. Back into the water he dove; this time when he resurfaced, he was carrying a huge load of the lost goods that had sunk to the bottom. He did this repeatedly until all was recovered.

Yao thanked him. "Not only have you saved my life," he said, "you have also restored my lost goods." And he began to believe that his companion was something more than human.

Now that the danger was past, the stranger wished to take his leave; but Yao implored him to stay, and the stranger finally agreed. Yao went through his goods and in the end determined that everything had been recovered save for a little gold pin. At once his companion plunged back into the water. The minutes passed, then up popped the stranger with the pin between his teeth. Those who had witnessed these events from shore were struck with amazement.

Yao returned home along with his companion, and they lived quite contentedly for a time. Every couple of months the big man would have a meal of incredible proportions, but eat nothing between.

❧

One day, as the sky darkened and the thunder rumbled ominously overhead, Yao said, "I wonder what the thunder is, and how the clouds carry the rain in their arms? Wouldn't it be wonderful to climb up to the sky and see?"

"Would you really like to wander among the clouds?" asked his companion later, as Yao was lying down to take a nap.

"Oh, yes," said Yao sleepily as he drifted off.

On awaking, he felt as if he were moving through the air rather than lying in his bed. He opened his eyes and found himself surrounded by clouds. He jumped up in great alarm and discovered the ground beneath his feet had gone as soft as cotton wool, so that he sank down in it. He felt dizzy – as if he were bobbing in a boat at sea. Above his head the stars looked like seeds in the cup of a lily, the largest ones the size of a huge basin, the smaller no bigger than a bowl. "Surely I must be dreaming," he thought, as he reached up on tiptoe and found that he could touch them. The larger ones were fixed, but he was able pluck one of the smallest, and tucked it up his sleeve.

Bending down, Yao parted the clouds beneath him.

Far below, the sea glittered like silver. Large cities looked no bigger than beans. "What a fall it would be should I happen to slip," he thought.

Just at that moment he heard a sound like the crack of a whip, and looking up, saw two dragons writhing through the clouds, drawing a cart behind them. The cart contained a great vat full of water, and a crew of men with buckets in their hands were busy drawing water and dousing the clouds with it. They were astonished to find Yao standing there, but one big fellow among them said, "It's all right. He's a friend of mine." So they handed Yao a bucket and he helped them with the water.

Now it happened that there had been a great drought in the land, and when Yao was given his bucket, he tried to dump his water so that it would all fall on his village. Presently his companion spoke to him: "I am an assistant to the Thunder God," he explained. "I had been exiled to the earth for three years for failing to perform my duties in sending down the rain. But now that time is up and I have returned, so we must part."

Then he took the long rope that served as the reins for the cart and told Yao to hold tight to one end, so that he might let him down to the earth. Yao was afraid, but his friend assured him there was no danger. He held on to the rope and – *whish-h-h-h* – in no time at all, he was back on solid ground. Up went the rope into the clouds, and he saw it no more.

It happened Yao had been let down just outside his village. A little rain had fallen all around to relieve the drought, but inside the village all the water courses were full. When he returned home, he took the star from his sleeve and set it on the table. During the day it looked like an ordinary stone, but by night it glowed brightly and lit up the whole house. It was a rare treasure, and Yao kept it carefully hidden away. He only brought it out when guests came over, to give them light while they were drinking wine.

※

After one such night, Yao's wife was sitting with him, combing out her hair, when suddenly the star dimmed and began to flit about the room like a firefly. Her mouth fell open in amazement and the star flew into it. Before she knew it, she had swallowed it, and no amount of coughing would coax it back up.

That night in his sleep Yao dreamt that his old friend Shia appeared before him and said, "I am the star Shao-wei. I have never forgotten your friendship, and now you have carried me back here from the sky. Truly our destinies are intertwined. And so it will continue, for in return for your kindness, I shall become your son."

Now, Yao was thirty years of age and without sons. But after this dream, his wife bore him a male child. Just before his birth, the room filled with light as it had when he set the star upon his table at night. So they called the child Star. He was extraordinarily brilliant, and by sixteen years of age had passed the official exams and taken his master's degree.

A Case of Possession

In Hu-nan Province there lived a woman whose husband was a trader and was often away on business. One night, while he was gone, the woman had a dream that there was someone in her room. Waking up, she searched the room and found a small creature that she recognized as a fox. But no sooner had she set eyes on it than the thing disappeared, though all the windows and the door were locked.

The following night she asked one of her maids to keep her company; her son too, a boy of about ten, came and slept in the room with her. In the middle of the night, when both the boy and the maid had fallen asleep, the fox came back. The maid was awakened by the sound of her mistress muttering to herself in her sleep. She called out and the fox ran off.

From that day there was something odd about the trader's wife. When night came she refused to blow out the candle, and she told her son to be sure not to sleep too soundly. But the boy and the maid fell asleep, and when they awakened they found the woman gone. They waited, but she did not return. The maid was far too frightened to go and look for her, but the son took a lamp and soon found his mother fast asleep in another room, though on waking she had no recollection of how she'd come there.

With each passing day, she grew stranger and stranger and she would have neither her son nor her maid keep her company anymore. However, the son kept watch over her, and if he heard any unusual sound, he would rush to her room, though she was bound to scold him for it.

※

One day he set to playing at being a stonemason. He began piling up stones on the windowsill, and if anyone dared to touch the stones, he would cause such a fuss that no one ventured near him. In a couple of days he had completely blocked up the windows with stones. He filled the chinks with mud where the light shone through. Then he went to the kitchen and put a keen edge on the chopper that he found there.

That night, he darkened his lamp and waited outside his mother's door. When she began to mutter in her sleep, he sprang up quickly, uncovered the light, and stood blocking the doorway.

"Who is there?" he cried. There was no answer, but as he advanced into the room a fox flashed out of the darkness and made for the door. The boy swung at it with the chopper and lopped off the end of its tail. Warm blood was still dripping from it as he shone the light upon it.

His mother, under the spell of the fox, cursed and reviled him for what he had done, but he paid her no mind, hoping only that he had frightened the creature off for good. The next morning he followed the trail of blood over the wall and into the garden of a neighboring family named Ho.

❧

That night, to his great joy, the fox did not return. His mother, meanwhile, remained in a strange stupor, hovering between life and death. It was at this time that the husband returned from his travels. His son told him all that had happened, at which he was greatly alarmed. He sent for a doctor immediately to examine his wife, but she cursed when he came near her, and when the doctor had gone she threw the medicines away. So the father and son secretly mixed the medicines in with her tea and soup, and within a few days she seemed better.

But one night the husband woke up and found her gone. He searched the house and discovered her sleeping in a closet. From then on she became increasingly eccentric, hiding herself away in strange places and giving grief to those who tried to remove her.

The husband was at his wit's end. It did no good keeping the door locked, for it opened of itself at her approach. And though he had called in any number of magicians, none of them were able to exorcise the fox.

※

One night his son hid himself in neighbor Ho's garden, where the trail of blood had led. The moon rose and he heard the sound of voices, and peeking from his hiding place in the long grass, he saw two men drinking while a long-bearded servant in an old brown coat waited upon them. They were talking together, but he could not make out what they saying. Except, as the two were rising to leave, one of them said to the servant, "Get some white wine for tomorrow."

When they had left, the servant took off his coat and lay down to sleep on the ground. At which the boy noticed that, while he appeared in all ways to be like a man, he had a tail. The boy was much too afraid to move lest he awaken the fox, so he stayed in hiding there until near dawn. Then the other two came back and, waking the third, they all three disappeared into the bushes.

※

"Where have you been all night?" asked his father when the boy returned home. But he said only that he had stayed the night at neighbor Ho's. Later that day the two went to town and, seeing a foxtail hanging in a hatter's window, the boy persuaded his father to buy it for him. While his father was making a purchase at another shop, the boy managed to take some money from his bag. Stealing off unseen, he bought some white wine, which he left in the wine merchant's care.

Now, in that town the boy had an uncle, a hunter by trade. And he asked his father if he might stop awhile on their way home and visit. As it happened, his uncle was out when he called, but his aunt was there, and pleased to see him.

"And how is your poor mother?" she inquired.

"Better these last few days," the boy replied. "But now she is all in a state, for a rat has gnawed at one of her dresses and ruined it. She wonders if you might have some poison."

"Indeed," said the aunt, and fetching some from the cupboard, she measured out a little and folded it into a piece of paper.

It seemed to him too little, so when she next left the room, he reached into the cupboard and fetched a full handful of the poison, wrapped it in paper, and put it in his pocket. Then he went to his aunt, who had started to prepare him something to eat. "Don't bother with that, Auntie," he said. "I must run along. Father is waiting for me in the marketplace." And off he went.

He wandered about the market for the rest of the afternoon and returned home near dark. The next day he did the same, and for some days following, until one day he saw among the crowd the long-bearded servant. He followed after him and managed to strike up a conversation, asking him where he lived.

"I live at Pei-ts'un," said the servant. "And you?"

"I live in a hole in the hillside," said the trader's son, falsely of course.

The long-bearded servant was taken aback by this answer, and more so when the boy added, "We've lived there for generations. Haven't *you*?"

The man asked him his name, to which the boy replied, "My name is Foxe. I saw you with two gentlemen in the garden of the Ho family not long back."

The long-bearded man, suspicious of the boy, was questioning him further, when the trader's son opened his coat a little so that the servant saw the end of the tail that the boy had bought at the hatter's shop.

"The likes of us can mix with ordinary people," said the boy. "But it's too bad we can't get rid of this."

The long-bearded man asked him what he was doing at the market, and the boy told him his father had sent him to buy wine.

"That's exactly what I'm here for," said the servant, whereupon the boy asked him if he had already bought it.

"We are quite poor," replied the servant. "I prefer to steal it."

"A dangerous business," said the boy.

"Indeed, but what is one to do? My masters have instructed me to get wine – and there is no money."

"And who might your masters be?" asked the boy.

"They are two brothers," replied the bearded man. "One of them has bewitched a lady named Wang; and the other, the wife of a trader who lives nearby. The son of that lady is a dangerous fellow. He lopped off the tip of my master's tail, so that he was laid up in bed for several days. But now he has the woman under his spell again. Well, enough talk, my friend; I must be off to fetch my wine."

"It's much easier to buy than to steal," said the boy. "I have some wine set aside at the wine-shop. You are more than welcome to it. I can always buy more."

"How can I ever thank you?"

"Don't mention it. We're all one family. And someday, when I'm in the neighborhood, I'll drop by and have a drink with you."

So off they went to the wine-shop. The boy gave the man the wine, and they went their separate ways.

❀

That night the boy's mother slept quietly, and the fits left her. The boy knew that something must have happened. He went to his father and told him everything, and together they went to neighbor Ho's to see what they would see.

They found the foxes lying dead on the grass, with an empty wine bottle between them. One of them bore the scar of a knife wound on its tail.

As they carried the dead foxes back home with them, the father asked his son why he had kept it all so secret.

"Foxes are the cunningest of creatures," said the boy. "They would doubtless have caught scent of the plot."

His father praised him. "Foxes may be cunning," said he, "but not nearly as cunning as you, my son."

From that day on they were left in peace. The trader's wife recovered her health, and her reason returned. The other woman, Mrs. Wang, was also freed from the fox's spell and took up her life again. As for the boy, he was taught riding and archery by his proud parents, and later rose to a high rank in the army.

A Supernatural Wife

Chao was a poor man who rented rooms with a family by the name of T'ai. He fell sick and his condition worsened, so that the family feared for his life. One day, they moved him onto the veranda, where the air was cooler. He slept fitfully and, on waking, was startled to find a beautiful young woman standing by his side.

"Who are you?" he asked.

"I have come to be your wife," she said.

"What would a beautiful young woman such as you want with a poor man like me?" he asked. "Besides, you must see that I am near death and have no need of a wife."

She told him then that she could cure him. He said that he doubted it, and even if she did prescribe him medicine, he had no means to pay for it.

"I have no need of medicines to cure you," she said. And she set about rubbing his back and sides with her hand. The touch of it was like fire against his skin, but he soon began to feel much better. He asked the young woman her name, that he might remember her in his prayers.

"I am a spirit," she said. "In a previous life you were a benefactor of my family. I have not forgotten that kindness, and have searched for you down the centuries that I might in some way repay you. Will you ask me in?"

"My poor rooms are not fit for one such as you," he pleaded. "The dirt will spoil your robe."

But at last he was persuaded to show her in. There were no chairs to sit on, and the cupboards all were bare.

"You see," he said. "How could I think of taking a wife? I have not even the means to support myself."

"Have no fear," she said. And in an instant the room was transformed. A couch covered with silken robes appeared and a long table laden with fine food and wine. The walls were hung with paper patterned with stars.

And so the two lived as husband and wife, while from all around the curious came to marvel at these strange things. And all were welcomed in to dine.

❧

One day among the company there was a young graduate with evil intent. The wife seemed to sense it straight off and began berating the stranger sternly. Then she cuffed him on the side of the head, and his head flew out the window while his body remained inside. There he stayed, stuck fast, unable either to come or to go, until the others interceded and the head and body were reunited.

A Supernatural Wife

In time the visitors became so numerous that the couple had no peace, and if the wife turned them away they grew angry with the husband.

It happened one day that the two were sitting drinking with friends during the Dragon-Boat Festival, when a rabbit ran into the room. Immediately the wife sprang up. "The doctor has come for me," she said, for tradition held that, at the foot of a cassia tree on the moon, there sat a rabbit who pounded out the drug from which the elixir of immortality was made. Turning to the rabbit, she said, "You go on and I'll follow."

The rabbit ran off, and the wife asked those assembled to fetch a ladder and set it against the tall tree in the garden. The top of the ladder overtopped the tree. The woman started up the ladder and Chao followed after her. She called out, urging anyone who wished to come to follow quickly. But no one save a serving boy from their house ventured after them. Up they climbed, higher and higher, until they disappeared from sight.

When the bystanders looked again at the ladder, they found it was only an old door-frame, with the panels knocked out. And when they went into Chao's rooms, they found them in the same filthy, unfurnished state as before. They determined to question the serving boy about it when he came back. But he never did.

The Pigeon Collector

Chang Kung-Liang collected pigeons. There are many varieties of pigeons, and he had patiently searched out and acquired them all – Boot Head, Big White, Black Stone, Love Bird, Puppy Eyes, and too many others to name. He even owned the rare Earth Star of Shansi, the Delicate Stork of Shan-tung, the Tumbler of Ho-nan, the Pointed Tips of Chekiang.

He cared for them as though they were his children. When it was cold, he fed them leaves and herbs; when it was hot, he gave them grains of salt. Pigeons like to sleep, but too much sleep can lead to death from palsy. So Chang purchased a small, energetic pigeon known as the Night Wanderer. He put it among his flock at night, and it would wander round and round without stopping, and ward off the palsy by keeping the other birds awake.

The Pigeon Collector

Chang took great pride in his collection, by far the best in Shan-tung.

❧

One night, as he was at work in his study, there came a knock on the door, and a young stranger dressed all in white entered the room.

"Who are you?" asked Chang.

"My name does not matter," replied the stranger. "I am a wanderer. The fame of your collection has reached me in a distant country. I, too, am a pigeon enthusiast, and I would very much like to see your birds."

"Certainly," said Chang, and he showed the young man his entire collection – birds of all colors and sizes.

"Your reputation is well deserved," said the stranger, when they were done. "I have a couple of my own birds nearby. Would you care to see them?"

Chang readily agreed. But as the stranger led him ever deeper into the deserted countryside, lit only by the misty moon, a sense of foreboding came upon him.

"It's not much farther now," said his companion, pointing into the darkness. "We shall soon be there."

And soon enough they came in sight of a Taoist retreat, a simple two-roomed hut surrounded by a courtyard. There was no lamp burning. The place was utterly dark. The young man took Chang by the hand and led him into the courtyard. He made a little cooing sound like a pigeon, and out of the window of the hut flew two snow-white pigeons. Up over the eaves and into the sky they soared, tumbling and swooping after one another, till at a sign from their master they flew off together.

Then he gave a peculiar whistle and two more pigeons emerged from the hut – one as large as a duck, the other no bigger than a man's fist. They began to dance upon the steps in imitation of storks. The larger craned its neck and spread its wings, cooing as it inclined this way and that to lead the other on, while the smaller bird flew up and down and finally alighted on the large bird's head. The shrill cries of the two blended in strange harmony, like the rhythmic striking of stone chimes. Then the smaller bird suddenly took flight, and the larger took up the dance again to lure it down.

Chang was beside himself with wonder, for he had never seen such a thing before. He begged the young man for some of these wonderful birds, but the stranger refused and shooed them away. Then he cooed as before and the two white pigeons appeared and flew down to him.

"You may have these, if you wish," he said, holding them out to Chang.

Chang took the pair from him. In the moonlight their eyes were like amber, the pitch black pupils round as peppercorns. When he stretched out their wings, he found that the flesh over their ribs was translucent and all the tiny organs could be seen couched within. He marveled at the birds, but still begged for others.

"I have more," said the stranger. "But I dare not show them to you now."

The Pigeon Collector

※

At that moment Chang's servants appeared on the road with torches, looking for him. When he turned back to the young man, he saw nothing but a white pigeon flying off into the night. As it vanished, so too did the hut and the courtyard, leaving only a small grave and a pair of cypress trees where he stood.

Chang was dumbstruck. The servants led him home, the two pigeons with him. They were very rare birds, and he tended them with great care. Two years later they hatched three cock pigeons and three females. Chang would not part with these, even to close relatives and friends.

But one day it chanced that a certain high official, a friend of his father's, asked him about his pigeons, and he decided that it might be in his interests to make the man a gift of a pair. He was hesitant to part with any of his favorites, but he could hardly offer ordinary pigeons to one so honored. So he took two of the prize white pigeons and presented them to him in a cage. They were a gift worth more than a thousand pieces of gold.

The next time he met the official, he was surprised to receive not a word of thanks. Finally, he asked him outright: "How did you like my birds?"

"They were delicious. Nice and plump and tasty."

"You don't mean that you ate them?"

"Why, of course."

"Those were no ordinary pigeons," said Chang, in horror. "They were the rarest of rare birds."

The official thought for a moment. "They didn't taste much different," he said.

Chang was greatly distressed.

That night the young man in white appeared to him in a dream. "I left my little ones in your care. How could you cast such pearls away? You allowed them to be killed and eaten! I shall take my children back now." Thereupon, he transformed himself into a pigeon, and with a cry, Chang's white pigeons followed after him.

When he looked for them the next morning, Chang found that his prize birds were gone. He was broken-hearted. He dispersed the remaining birds among his friends within a few days. For the remainder of his life he collected no more.

The Arrival of the Buddhist Monks

One day two Buddhist monks arrived in our country from the West. Their clothes and their complexions, their language and their features were much different from those of our country. They were full of travelers' tales. They said they had crossed the Fiery Mountains, where smoke streamed perpetually from the peaks as from the chimney of a furnace. It was only safe to travel there after the rain, when the ground was cool enough to walk upon. And even then one had to proceed with extreme caution, for flames would shoot from the ground if so much as a stone was dislodged.

The monks also said they had passed through the River of Sand, from the midst of which rose a cliff of pure crystal, whose sheer face was utterly transparent. The only way past was through a narrow gorge, guarded by two dragons with crossed horns. Those who wished to pass had to bow and beg permission of these dragons, and if it was granted, the horns would open and let them through. These dragons were white, and their scales shone like crystal as they moved.

The monks had been on the road for eighteen winters and eighteen summers. Of the twelve that had embarked upon the journey together, only two had reached China. They said that, in their country, China is famed for its mountains, and the people there believe that our streets are paved with gold. They believe that Kuan-yin, the goddess of Mercy, and Wen-shu, the god of Wisdom, dwell here upon the earth, and that they need only journey here to ensure immortality and attain Buddhahood.

Hearing these things, it struck me that this was exactly what our own people think about the West; and that if travelers from each country could only meet halfway and tell each other the true state of affairs, there would be hearty laughter on both sides, and much unnecessary trouble could be saved.

The Magic Path

In the province of Kuang-tung there lived a scholar named Kuo. One evening, while returning home from visiting a friend, he lost his way among the hills. He wandered aimlessly in a deep wood for hours. Then suddenly he heard talking and laughing from the top of a hill. He hurried in the direction of the sound and came upon a dozen men sitting on the ground drinking.

"Come along," they said, as they caught sight of him. "There's always room for one more."

So Kuo came and sat down with them. He noticed that they were all dressed as scholars. "I wonder if you could direct my way home from here?" he asked.

"A fine fellow you are," said one of them, "bothering about the way home, with such a fine moon as this tonight." And he handed him a cup of wine. Kuo drank it all in one swallow, and another of the company immediately filled his cup again. Being thirsty from his long walk, he drank that one down as well. And so it went. In no time at all, he'd no more thought of the way home, and was full of fun.

Now, it so happened that Kuo was a great mimic, and could imitate the song of any bird. As he wandered off to relieve himself, he began twittering on the sly, like a swallow.

"How is it that the swallow sings so late?" wondered one of the company, and they looked about them, astonished, much to Kuo's amusement.

Then he began to imitate the song of the cuckoo, and their wonder increased. He sat back down with them, laughing to himself as his companions discussed the extraordinary sounds they had heard. After a while, he began making noises like a parrot, saying, "Mr. Kuo is drunk. It is time to take him home."

They were all astounded. They listened intently, but there was only silence. Then the parrot spoke again. But this time they discovered the trick, and they all burst out laughing. They twisted up their mouths and tried to imitate Kuo, but none of them could do it.

❧

"What a pity Madam Ching isn't here with us," one of them observed after a time. "We will meet here again at midautumn, Mr. Kuo, and you must be sure to join us."

Kuo promised he would. Then one of the men stood and said that, since Kuo had offered them such amusing entertainment, they would show him some of their acrobatic accomplishments.

They all stood up. One of them planted his feet firmly on the ground, and a second jumped onto his shoulders. Then a third jumped onto the second's shoulders, and a fourth onto his. It was too high then for the rest to jump up, so they began to scramble up as if they were scaling a ladder. In no time at all, they were all up, and the head of the topmost seemed to touch the stars.

Then the whole column bent gradually down until it lay along the ground, transformed into a path. Kuo stood there for a long while, struck with wonder. Then, starting along the path, he was soon home.

Some days later, he revisited the spot. There were dense bushes everywhere, and in a little clearing, the remains of a feast scattered on the ground. Yet nowhere was there a sign of a path.

As midautumn came around, Kuo thought about keeping his engagement. But his friends persuaded him not to go.

The Painted Wall

One day chance led Chu and his friend Meng to an old monastery. There were no spacious halls or meditation chambers, but an old monk greeted them at the door and showed them what there was to be seen.

In the chapel there stood a statue of the Buddha, and the walls on all sides round were painted with images of men and beasts. On the east wall was a painting of a group of fairies, picking flowers on a green hillside. Among them was one girl with her hair unbound. She was smiling and her red lips seemed about to move.

Chu stood looking at the girl for a long while, and suddenly he felt as though he were floating through the air. In an instant he had passed with ease into the wall. He found himself seated with a crowd, listening while an old monk preached the law of Buddha.

Suddenly he felt a tug on his sleeve. Glancing around,

he saw the girl who had been picking flowers in the painting. She walked away, laughing, and he followed after her. She led him down a narrow street to a house, where she went in. Passing up a winding stair, she came to the door of an apartment. Chu was afraid to go further, but she waved the flowers in her hand as if beckoning him in.

He entered and found the place empty but for them. She kissed him then, and they fell into a long embrace.

The days passed in bliss. From time to time the girl went away and bade him be quiet until she returned. But her companions soon caught on to the secret and discovered Chu hidden in her room.

They laughed and said, "My dear, you are no longer a girl. You are a woman now. You must bind your hair."

They brought her the proper hairpins and head ornaments, and she fashioned her hair into a high topknot, with a coronet of pendants.

Then one of them cried, "Let's be off and leave these lovebirds alone." And they left the room.

Now, as the two sat together, suddenly they heard a sound on the stairs like the tramping of heavy boots and the clanking of chains. There was a great shouting, so they sprang up in fear and peeked through a crack in the door. And they saw a fierce-looking man clad from head to toe in golden armor, carrying a golden chain.

"Are you all here?" he demanded, as the girls gathered around him.

"Yes, all," they said.

"If any mortal be hidden among you, denounce him at once or grief will come upon you."

But they swore there was no one.

Still, the man said he would search the place. When Chu's beloved heard this, her face turned the color of ash. In her terror, she turned to him and said, "Hide yourself under the bed." And opening a small lattice in the wall, she disappeared.

Chu lay under the bed, barely daring to breathe, while outside the door of the room there was a sound of voices going back and forth through the apartment. Suddenly the door was flung open, and heavy boots tramped across the floor. He lay completely still, pressed up close against the wall. His ears began to sing, his eyes to burn like fire. At last the footsteps withdrew. He listened to them fade away into the house.

❧

Meanwhile, back in the monastery chapel, Meng had noticed his friend's sudden disappearance and asked the old monk where he had gone.

"He has gone to hear the preaching of the law," said the monk.

"But where?"

"Not far," said the monk, and he tapped twice on the wall and called out: "Friend, what makes you stay away so long?"

Suddenly a great noise like the sound of thunder filled the room where Chu lay. He sprang out in terror from under the bed . . .

The Painted Wall

... And found himself standing again in the monastery chapel with Meng and the old monk. Meng took one look at his trembling friend and begged Chu to tell him where he had been and what was the matter.

But Chu was staring at the picture painted on the wall of the fairies gathering flowers. And Meng saw that the girl whose hair had hung loose now wore it bound in a high topknot, with a coronet of pendants about her forehead.

The friends were astonished at the sight and asked the monk what it could mean.

"Visions have their origins in those who see them," said the monk. "What explanation can I give?"

The friends could make no sense of the monk's reply. Full of fear and wonder, they slowly descended the monastery steps and went upon their way.

The End.